T5-CRC-837

THE MYSTERY MACHINE

ALSO BY HERBIE BRENNAN

EMILY AND THE WEREWOLF
illustrated by David Pace

THE MYSTERY MACHINE

HERBIE BRENNAN

Margaret K. McElderry Books

FOR SIAN, WITH MY LOVE

Margaret K. McElderry Books
An imprint of Simon & Schuster Children's Publishing Division
1230 Avenue of the Americas
New York, New York 10020

Designed by Nancy Williams
The text of this book is set in Aldine 721 BT.
Printed in the United States of America
First edition
10 9 8 7 6 5 4 3 2 1

Library of Congress Cataloging-in-Publication Data
Brennan, Herbie.
    The mystery machine / by Herbie Brennan — 1st ed.   p.   cm.
    Summary: Hubert accidentally discovers that the weird woman who moved
in next door is really a member of an alien race that plans to take over Earth.
    ISBN 0-689-50615-5
    [1. Extraterrestrial beings—Fiction. 2. Science Fiction.]   I. Title
PZ7.B75153My   1994
[Fic]—dc20   94-4185

J

CHAPTER ONE

"What's the matter?" Hubert asked, although he didn't really want to know.

His cousin Janice, who was sitting on a pile of earth behind the rose bush, stopped sobbing long enough to look up. When she saw it was Hubert, she started sobbing again.

"Come on . . ." Hubert said uneasily. His hands moved in nervous circles as he wondered if he should put an arm around her shoulders. He decided against it. For several days now, he had been prey to a dreadful suspicion that she might be in love with him, and he didn't want to encourage it. "Come on . . ." he said again.

"It was awful!" Janice gasped at last. "That *pukey* woman!"

"What was awful?" Hubert asked sympathetically. "Which pukey woman?" He squatted down beside her, sitting on his schoolbag to protect the seat of his pants. Janice, he noticed, had got earth all over her dress.

"Mrs. Pomfrey-Parkinson!" Janice exclaimed between renewed sobs.

"Oh, *that* pukey woman," Hubert said. He'd been hearing a lot lately about Mrs. Pomfrey-Parkinson, who seemed to be a snob and a bully. She had moved into the semidetached house next door very recently, but already half the kids in the village hated her. He wondered what she'd done to Janice, who lived two streets away.

"She hit me!" Janice told him shrilly. She held the back of her hand out to him with the air of one displaying a bleeding wound.

Hubert stared at the hand. There was no sign of any injury whatsoever. "What did you do?" he asked suspiciously.

Janice stopped crying to look at him in wide-eyed amazement. "I didn't do *anything*." Hubert stared at her without speaking until she added sullenly, "I was just minding my own business in her garden."

"In her garden," Hubert echoed. He sighed. "She told you not to come into her garden." Mrs. Pomfrey-Parkinson had told every kid in the neighborhood not to come into her garden.

"Yes," Janice agreed, "but there was no need to *hit* me." She sniffed.

"What were you doing in her garden anyway?" Hubert asked. He didn't want to prolong this. There was a circus coming to Pugford and he was trying to figure out a way of persuading his father to fork out the price of admission. It was not going to be easy. But still, he was curious about what had happened to Janice.

"I just went in to say hello to Hassle," Janice mumbled. She was quite a pretty girl, but two years younger than he was. He found kids that age boring, especially girls.

"She's *told* you not to do that," he said unsympathetically.

Hassle was Mrs. Pomfrey-Parkinson's dog, a scruffy mongrel with a lot more personality than his owner. He was a firm favorite of the local children, all of whom had been warned not to come into Mrs. Pomfrey-Parkinson's garden to pet him.

"I know, but I *love* Hassle!" Janice protested. She gave Hubert a sidelong look as if suggesting Hassle wasn't the only one she loved.

Hubert ignored it. "What happened?"

Janice shrugged. "She caught me."

"And hit you?"

Something in his voice made Janice glance away. "Well, she *nearly* hit me."

"Nearly?"

"She shook her fist at me," Janice said angrily. "She made *threatening gestures!*"

Hubert climbed to his feet. Like most of Janice's complaints, this one had sprung a leak. He didn't know why he bothered to talk to her. When it came right down to it, she never had anything really interesting to say.

Suddenly Janice did say something interesting. "I think she's a witch."

Hubert stopped. Something in his cousin's voice made him turn around. He stared at Janice.

"I mean," Janice said, "she really *is* a witch."

"There aren't any such things," Hubert told her. Actually he was a bit confused about witches.

His parents had told him long ago there were no such things, but every so often he saw stuff in the Sunday papers with headlines like: WITCHES HORROR PROBE.

"Yes, there are!" Janice said with fearsome certainty. "And she's one. I saw her eyes flash red."

Hubert stared at her blankly. It occurred to him he'd been doing quite a lot of staring during this brief conversation.

"Like in the movies," Janice said. She obviously took his stare for disbelief, for she added urgently, "They really did."

"There's no such thing as witches," Hubert repeated. He tended to believe red-flashing eyes were just a camera trick, but he didn't want to get into that. He turned back again to the house.

"Will you get her for me?" Janice asked suddenly. Her face had taken on an enthusiastic grimace.

Hubert stopped. "Get her?"

"Beat her up!" said Janice eagerly. "Make her leave home! Send her away. And while you're at it, you might get her to give me Hassle."

"Me?" asked Hubert, appalled. "Why don't you? You're the one who thinks she's a witch. You're the one she made the *threatening gestures* to."

"There's no need to be sarcastic," Janice told him huffily. "Boys are supposed to protect girls—my mother told me."

Hubert doubted Janice's mother had told her anything of the sort. Janice's mother wore jeans and a T-shirt with a clenched fist printed on the front. But Janice read a lot and he had twice seen her carrying books about dragons, knights, and maidens. He turned toward his home again. He could see his father through the window straightening a picture in the living room. The car was in the driveway, which meant his mother must be back from shopping. "Well, I'm not going to," he said over his shoulder. As an afterthought he added, "You'd better go home—there's mud on your dress."

Janice started to cry again as he walked toward the front door, but he ignored her. He had far too many problems of his own without taking on somebody else's.

CHAPTER TWO

Hubert walked directly to the kitchen and poured himself a glass of orange juice from the refrigerator. Getting money from his father was like pulling teeth from a dinosaur, and he felt the need of fortification. By the time he'd finished his juice and wandered back toward the living room, he could tell from the raised voices that his parents were having a fight, but he went in anyway.

"Not—" his father was saying with exaggerated clarity and patience "—my—fault!"

"Whose fault is it, then?" Hubert's mother asked. She glanced around as Hubert came in and promptly seized him as an ally. "Look," she said, angrily. She pointed. "Look at that!"

Hubert took a mental line of sight along her finger and ended up looking at the hearth rug. He wondered why it was being brought to his attention. It was definitely not a new one, but perhaps she'd had the old one cleaned. She got very edgy when she did things around the house and neither he nor his dad noticed. Maybe that was what the fight was all about. Except that the hearth rug didn't look as if it had been cleaned. If anything, it looked pretty dirty. He was aware he was running out of time. He wondered if he should say something positive, but nonspecific like, "Well done," and then take it from there.

"Well," his mother said, her tone an octave higher, "*say* something!"

Something told him "Well done" might be off target, so he pursed his lips, frowned and murmured, "Mmm."

His mother swung around on his father again. "You see?" she said. "Even Hubert notices and heaven knows he doesn't notice much. That's how bad it is."

"Not—" Hubert's father began again "—my—"

"Don't keep repeating things like a parrot," Hubert's mother warned him. "The reason that rug's filthy is the state of the chimney. And the state of the chimney is because it hasn't been swept. And it hasn't been swept because you, Arnold, *are too cheap to call the chimney sweep!!*"

"Steady, Madge," Hubert's father said, falling back a step or two.

"Don't you steady me, Arnold Baker," Hubert's mother screamed furiously. "If I have to clean that up just once more, just *once* more, I shall leave home!" She tossed her head so her hair bounced threateningly and stormed from the room.

"Soot on the hearth rug," Hubert's father explained in the silence that followed. He stared ruefully at the offending floor covering. "Your mother wants something done about it."

Hubert came over and peered down at the hearth rug. Now that he knew what he was looking for, he could see the soot quite clearly. It was the remains of a fall from the chimney that had left soot in the hearth and on the tiles surrounding it. There was even a speck or two beyond the hearth rug on the carpet. "I'll get the vacuum cleaner," Hubert said. Normally he would not have touched the vacuum cleaner, but he had a feeling if there was any hope at all of circus money it might depend on extraordinarily good behavior.

He glanced out of the kitchen window as he was dragging the vacuum cleaner from its cupboard and saw the car was now missing from the driveway. As he walked back into the living room he said, "I think Mom's off to the boutique."

His father sat down on the couch and groaned. He held his head in his hands and groaned again. Hubert knew what he was thinking. Every time his wife got upset, she headed for the boutique and bought something unbelievably expensive.

Hubert plugged in the vacuum and switched on the power. It was the hose and nozzle type and since a brush head would only work soot into the carpet he did not fit one on. Instead he crept up on the little pile with the hose itself. At a distance of six inches, the soot abruptly disappeared into the hose. There was no mark on the carpet underneath.

He moved on to the hearth rug and made the soot there disappear as well. This time he was not so lucky—the rug still looked decidedly grubby.

He moved the hose closer and the rug rose to meet it, trying to wriggle all the way inside the vacuum cleaner hose. The motor changed note and began to strain. Hubert jerked the nozzle away, freed the rug, and spread it smooth again. It still looked grubby. He decided to leave well enough alone and moved on to vacuum up the soot in the fireplace. When he had finished, he turned to his father, planning to say something like, "There—all clean. Mom will calm down now. Any chance of money for the circus?" His father's lips were moving.

Hubert switched off the vacuum cleaner. "What?" he asked.

"Women don't appreciate money," repeated Hubert's father, who appreciated money more than anything else on earth. "Your mother, for instance."

"I know," Hubert said sympathetically. He thought if he showed enough sympathy there was a chance—a small chance, but a chance—his father just might cough up the money for the circus.

"Take this business about the soot," his father said miserably. "She wants the chimney cleaned. Have you any idea how much it costs to call a chimney sweep these days?"

"No, Dad," Hubert said. He leaned forward to give the impression he was hanging on every word.

"Eleven pounds!" his father exploded. His eyes widened in shock and astonishment at the amount. "When I was a boy, a sweep cost half a crown."

Hubert allowed his own eyes to widen in shock and astonishment. "Eleven pounds!" he echoed. "Why you could buy *groceries* for eleven pounds. You could buy *shoes* for eleven pounds." He set his face into a sober mask and added cunningly, "You could go to the *circus* for eleven pounds." He watched his father closely, trying to gauge his reactions. He licked his lips. "Speaking of circuses, there's one coming to town next weekend. . . ."

"Your mother thinks I'm made of money," his father said gloomily. "Eleven pounds! And now she's off to that boutique"—he made it sound like the town dump—"to run up bills on my credit card." His face took on the expression of one who is having a foot amputated. "I have no control over her, Hubert. And the money just goes. It just disappears."

"And I was wondering," Hubert went on,

rolling his eyes casually toward the heavens, "if you could possibly let me have a little pocket money so I could go?"

His father's mouth snapped shut like a trap. "Are you out of your mind?" he asked.

CHAPTER THREE

After he had polished off his supper and his homework, Hubert changed into shorts and went out to kick a soccer ball to work off some of his frustrations. Since he was not allowed to play on the lawn, he used the rough ground at the bottom of the back garden. The trees made kicking difficult and sort of interesting.

With his mind on other things, he dropped the ball on his foot and kicked. The ball described a high, slow arc, crossed the boundary fence, and dropped like a death knell into Mrs. Pomfrey-Parkinson's garden. Hubert stared after it in openmouthed disbelief.

After a moment, he gathered himself together. It was no big deal—he'd just slip into Mrs. Pomfrey-Parkinson's garden and get his ball back. How much trouble could that be?

He hesitated. Mrs. Pomfrey-Parkinson was supposed to be bad tempered, loud, violent, evil-minded, unreasonable, and stupid. No wonder Janice thought she was a witch. But he'd never actually spoken to her. He'd certainly seen her—she was a stout woman who moved in a cloud of perfume and looked as if she should be wearing a fur coat all the time—but everything else he knew about her came from other kids. Maybe they were just exaggerating how bad she was.

He still hesitated. Something inside told him they were not exaggerating.

Hubert looked down at his foot—the one that had kicked the ball. He was being silly. After all, he was only going to slip into Mrs. Pomfrey-Parkinson's garden to get back his own property. She couldn't possibly object to that. If she even noticed him. He would be in and out in seconds. He would zip in, grab his soccer ball, then zip out again. She wouldn't even have time to notice him.

The thought made him feel better. Then he had another thought that made him feel better still. Mrs. Pomfrey-Parkinson might be out. He walked to the fence, stood on tiptoe, and peered over. There was no sign of her car in the drive. She had a garage and the car might be tucked away in there, but most of the time she left it out. Hubert felt a grin beginning to crawl across his face. It looked as if he could have gotten lucky.

With the thought that Mrs. Pomfrey-Parkinson might be out came the thought that she might also be coming back, which added a certain urgency to the whole operation. So did the fact that Mrs. Pomfrey-Parkinson kept her back gate locked, which meant you could only get into her back garden by going around to the front. Hubert hurried to the front.

Mrs. Pomfrey-Parkinson's house was almost a twin of his own, semidetached, sharing the same middle wall, but divided at the front by a high hedge instead of a fence. One difference was there were two entrances to Mrs. Pomfrey-Parkinson's property: a driveway further along and a pedestrian path with a little wooden gate. Hubert headed for the wooden gate. There were high bushes and less chance of being seen. He crept through the small front garden (where Janice had presumably been caught, his mind mentioned uneasily), along the side of her house, and into her back garden. He felt like a scout pushing deep into enemy territory.

Mrs. Pomfrey-Parkinson's garden was a lot nicer to look at than his father's, but this was no credit to Mrs. Pomfrey-Parkinson, who only ever came out to shout at children. The garden had been laid out by the previous owner, an elderly gentleman named Mr. Willis, who had died gently, while tending to his roses. Since Mr. Willis had no immediate family, the house was put up for sale by his lawyers. Mrs. Pomfrey-Parkinson bought it and the money went to a distant cousin in Australia.

Hubert let his gaze sweep across the back lawn and flower beds. There was no sign of his soccer ball. After a moment, he crept out from the shadow of the bushes and moved a little further along the path. There was still no sign of his soccer ball, but thankfully there was no sign of Mrs. Pomfrey-Parkinson either. He became more certain by the minute that she had gone out. All the same, he still felt nervous.

He tried to estimate where the ball would have come over the fence, which wasn't really very difficult. Then he tried to imagine where it might have rolled to, which was. His best guess was a rosebush. But inspecting the rosebushes would leave him in clear sight of Mrs. Pomfrey-Parkinson's living-room window. Hubert hesitated. Did he dare risk it? Risk what? a voice asked in his head. You've already decided she's gone out. But I could be wrong about that, Hubert told the voice.

But if he was wrong, what difference would it make? He was, he reminded himself, only getting his own property. He wasn't a burglar, or a vandal. He wasn't going to hurt her rosebushes. He was just going to zip over, grab the soccer ball, and zip off again.

Hubert zipped over, one eye on Mrs. Pomfrey-Parkinson's living-room window. Net curtains obscured his view inside, but at least the curtains didn't twitch. For some reason he kept thinking of Janice saying Mrs. Pomfrey-Parkinson was a witch. Not that he believed it. Not at all.

He reached the rosebushes. There was no sign of his soccer ball anywhere near them. He dropped to his knees and peered under the bushes.

It was difficult to see, but there was a sort of tunnel that a soccer ball might have rolled into. He crawled forward and stuck his head into the tunnel. If she really was a witch, this was a dreadful situation to be caught in. He had his head underneath a rosebush, his legs sticking out, and his rear end up in the air. As he strained to see a soccer ball in the gloom beneath a rosebush, he could not stop imagining Mrs. Pomfrey-Parkinson slowly creeping up behind him. She was dressed in a black robe with a black pointed hat. She carried a broom in one hand and a fat, slimy, warty toad in the other.

It was the toad that worried Hubert most. He imagined it cold and horrible and poisonous, dripping with green slime. He told himself it was nonsense, but he kept imagining it just the same. He kept seeing Mrs. Pomfrey-Parkinson reaching out with that dreadful toad in her hand, ready to drop it on his upturned rear end. Nonsense, of course, but—

There was a small noise, then something cold and slimy touched his bare leg just behind the knee. Hubert screamed and backed out of the rosebushes at ninety miles an hour. Mrs. Pomfrey-Parkinson's scruffy mongrel Hassle jumped back in alarm. He cocked his head to look at Hubert and gave a tiny *Woof*.

Hubert flopped over on the grass. He felt light-headed with relief. "Hassle," he gasped. "You scared the life out of me!" Hassle wagged his tail. When he caught his breath, Hubert said, "Have you seen a soccer ball around here anywhere, Hassle?" He climbed to his feet. The ball was definitely not under the rosebushes. He wondered vaguely if Hassle might have carried it off, but decided it was a bit big for the little fellow to grip in his mouth. He looked around. If it hadn't gone under the rosebushes, it must have rolled past them. Which would take it . . .

Hubert followed the direction the ball must have taken and discovered there was a garden shed half hidden by some trees beyond the rosebushes. It looked new, and since he hadn't remembered it in Mr. Willis's day, he supposed Mrs. Pomfrey-Parkinson must have had it built. The shed door was shut, but the window was open, so the ball might—just might—be inside.

He felt a shiver down his spine as he started forward. What worried him was what Mrs. Pomfrey-Parkinson would do if she found him creeping around inside her shed. But he quickly discovered he would not be creeping around anywhere. The shed door was locked.

Hubert stared for a moment, wondering why Mrs. Pomfrey-Parkinson would want to lock away a few old gardening tools. But he decided it was none of his business. All he wanted was his soccer ball. If it was inside, he would have to climb through the window to get it.

The window was too high for him to look through. He glanced around. He was feeling about as nervous as he had ever been in his life. The prospect of Mrs. Pomfrey-Parkinson finding him in her garden shed was so terrifying he could hear his heart thumping. Maybe he would be better off just asking Mrs. Pomfrey-Parkinson to give him back his ball. He might even do it by phone or letter so he wouldn't have to come into this dreadful garden again. The only thing was, he had to be sure the ball was in the shed.

Hubert took a deep breath and jumped to catch the windowsill. He pulled himself upward with difficulty until his chin was level with the bottom of the open window.

There were very few garden tools in the shed, hardly any at all. Instead, it was almost filled, floor to ceiling, with the weirdest piece of machinery he had ever seen. He had a glimpse of gleaming tubes and glistening panels, snaking cables, and what looked like a massive bank of flashing lights. The whole thing gave off a low-pitched hum that set his teeth on edge. Lying on the floor beside it was his soccer ball.

From behind him, Hassle growled softly.

Still hanging from the window, Hubert half turned his head. "Hush, you silly—" He stopped. Beyond Hassle, Mrs. Pomfrey-Parkinson was bearing down across the lawn, moving faster than he would ever have believed possible for a woman of her bulk.

She waved her arms about like tentacles so that he suddenly realized exactly what Janice had meant by *threatening gestures*. He could even, in that instant, believe she might really be a witch. There was something about the woman that was absolutely terrifying. "What," she shouted furiously, her voice cracking with rage, "do you think you're doing?"

Hubert knew exactly what he was doing. He was dropping from the shed and running like a maniac back up the side of the house and out of the garden. She could keep his stupid ball for all he cared. All he wanted was to get away. He careered through the little front gate, ran down the street, and vaulted the gate of his own front garden without taking time to open it. He did not stop running until he was safely in the kitchen of his own home. He watched for nearly five minutes through the kitchen window before he was completely satisfied that Mrs. Pomfrey-Parkinson had not followed. His racing heart began slowly to return to normal.

Still panting slightly, Hubert walked over to the refrigerator in the hope of finding yogurt to ward off the possibility of shock. But as he opened the door, he realized something that almost made him lose his appetite. Janice had been right. When Mrs. Pomfrey-Parkinson bore down on him, her eyes had definitely flashed red.

CHAPTER FOUR

Hubert climbed onto the bus, stowed his school-bag on the overhead rack, and collapsed grate-fully into a seat beside a lady reading the *Pugford Chronicle*. He usually sat at the back with his friends, but he had nearly missed the bus, and this was the only seat available. He turned and waved to Slider Coffrey, who was sandwiched between two girls and wore a smug look on his face. He had his lunch box open and was eating a corned-beef sandwich, even though it was only just past breakfast time. But that was nothing unusual for Slider.

Hubert turned back and stared out the window. The reason he'd nearly missed the bus was that he'd slept late. The reason he'd slept late was that he'd lain awake through half the night, thinking about his soccer ball and reliving the terrifying flight from Mrs. Pomfrey-Parkinson. So here he was in the morning, exhausted from lack of sleep, minus his only soccer ball, and still no nearer to figuring out a way of getting to the circus. There were times when life was hardly worth the effort.

The bus ride to school took twenty minutes, and he normally passed the time talking to his friends. Today, well separated from them, he had to content himself with looking out the window and examining his fellow passengers. Neither provided much inspiration. His eyes drifted over the copy of the *Chronicle* the lady beside him was reading. On the back page, the Pugford Rovers had dropped to the bottom of the Junior Soccer League. On the front, a special meeting of the Pugford District Council had shelved a new traffic plan. He stifled a yawn.

Then, toward the bottom of page one, he

caught sight of a two-column headline: HUMAN CANNONBALL FIRED. His interest was aroused at once. He squinted to read the small type and discovered that the Great Cascardi, a human cannonball for more than thirty years, had been dismissed from the circus when he got too fat to fit into the gun. It was difficult to finish the story because of the way the newspaper was folded, but Hubert leaned across and twisted his head until he managed it. Cascardi, it seemed, had taken dismissal philosophically: He had planned to retire next year anyway. The circus management was now looking for someone to replace him.

The lady lowered her paper and glared at Hubert, whose head was now almost on her lap. He straightened up hurriedly and gave her a nervous smile. "Sorry," he said. He wondered if he should ask to borrow the paper, but decided against it. He'd read the whole story anyway. His stomach was aflame with excitement. This was how he could get to see the circus! And from the inside. All his life he'd dreamed about performing, and here was his chance.

He leaned back and closed his eyes, listening to the cheers and applause. He could see himself quite plainly, dressed in sinister black leather and a motorcycle helmet. Across the front of his chest was emblazoned the image of a huge explosion, yellow rimmed with red. In the middle of the explosion were the words:

The Great Huberto
Human Cannonball

What he really wanted to see was *The Great Huberto, Youngest Human Cannonball on Earth,* but even in his imagination he was having trouble making it fit. But it didn't matter. Everybody could see how young he was. Everybody could appreciate his daring.

You know your parents won't allow this, the voice of reason muttered sourly in his head. Hubert clung stubbornly to his picture. He knew his parents would never allow it, but that didn't matter. He knew he was too young to leave school, but that didn't matter either. If he could give even one performance as a human cannonball, that would be enough. He would have his moment of glory and, as a bonus, get to see the rest of the circus for free.

So his parents were no problem—they'd never know about it until it was all over. School was no problem—the circus played in Pugford on the weekend. The only problem he could really see was how to convince the circus management he knew all about being a human cannonball.

He was still wrestling with that one as he got off the bus and fell into step beside Slider. By way of bringing up the topic he asked, "Do you know anything about the circus that's coming on the weekend?"

"They do great popcorn," Slider said.

"Do they? How do you know?"

"Circuses always do great popcorn."

"Do they?" Hubert took a deep breath. "They're looking for a human cannonball."

"Really?" Slider said, adding, "You don't want to go to the cafeteria for lunch today—they're serving semolina pudding for dessert. Why don't you come to Cafolla's with me? We could have thick milkshakes and potato chips." Cafolla's was the local café. Slider was obviously not interested in the circus.

"No money," Hubert told him shortly, not for the first time. Casually he added, "I was thinking of applying."

"At Cafolla's?" Slider looked genuinely bewildered.

"No, the human cannonball thing."

"Have you done it before?" Slider asked.

Hubert shook his head.

"They won't give you the job if you haven't done it before," Slider said. He warmed suddenly to his theme. "Circuses are just the same as any other business, you know. People think they're different because of all the costumes and the music and the elephants, but they aren't. They're run by accountants nowadays, just like everything else. You wouldn't expect to get a job in, say, a lawyer's office without experience. It's the same with a circus." They turned in at the school gate and began to push through the melee in the yard. "Does your old man know you're going to join the circus?"

"I haven't told him," Hubert said. "Actually I've only just thought of it." They shouldered the swing door open and entered the school building. "Do you really think they won't give me the job without experience? It's only getting shot out of a cannon. All you have to do is lie there and wait with your fingers in your ears."

"They still won't let you do it unless you've done it before," Slider said knowledgeably. He dropped his schoolbag beside his locker and started fishing for his key. "Of course, we can do something about that."

"We can?" Hubert asked. One of the things he liked about Slider was his ingenuity. Another was his confidence.

Slider nodded. "No problem—I'll see you around at your place after supper."

CHAPTER FIVE

There was, thank heaven, no sign of Janice in the garden when Hubert came home from school that day. The car was gone from the drive, and for a moment he thought he might actually have the house to himself. But when he rambled around to the back door, he noticed their aluminum ladder and the tube of rods used to clean drains propped against the wall, which almost certainly meant someone was at home. He discovered his father seated at the kitchen table, his head in his hands.

"Hi, Dad," Hubert said as he headed for the refrigerator.

His father groaned.

Hubert stopped. "What's the matter, Dad?"

His father looked up. His face was streaked with dirt and his hands were filthy. His eyes were red and puffy as if he had been crying. "She's gone!" he moaned.

Hubert looked at him blankly.

"Your mother," his father said. "She's left me—us. Packed her bags, took the car, and went. She's even taken Tiddles."

It occurred to Hubert there was a bright side to every tragedy. He'd hated that cat since the first time it peed on his homework. All the same, it was a shock to find his mother gone without so much as a fond good-bye. "What happened?" he gasped.

"Soot," his father said. "Soot on the carpet."

This time Hubert groaned. He turned back to the refrigerator and poured himself a glass of orange juice. He noticed there was very little left in the carton and suspected it would be a long time before he would be drinking any more: If his father was going to do the shopping, they'd probably live on baked beans.

"I should have known," his father said. "I should have listened to her. Women go insane when they see soot on the carpet. She said she was going to leave home if it happened again, and it did, and she did." He stared bleakly into space. "We may never see my beloved again."

"Where's she gone?" Hubert asked.

"Home to her mother. Imagine how miserable she must be."

Hubert found it difficult. His grandmother, who lived in a large house outside Meresdon, had been left a fortune by her husband when he died and was now sensibly trying to spend it all before *she* did. Visits to grandmother were one long series of expensive chocolates, fizzy drinks, and trips to any entertainments within twenty miles. For just the barest instant it occurred to him he should have asked her for a loan to go to the circus, but he dismissed the thought. His plan was still to become a human cannonball, and he had to maintain a positive mental attitude. Besides, he was in the middle of a domestic tragedy. To ease his father's grief he said, "Maybe she'll come back if we clean up the soot."

"I've already done that," his father said. He

held out his hands for inspection and gestured at his filthy face. Then his shoulders slumped. "I don't think it's going to be enough."

Neither did Hubert. The question of falling soot had caused arguments between his parents for as long as he could remember. The chimney had been swept three years ago and his father was so shocked by the cost that he hadn't had it done since. As gently as he could, Hubert suggested, "Maybe if you called a chimney sweep."

His father's expression changed at once from sorrow to outrage. "At eleven pounds a visit?" he exclaimed. His expression softened, then broke into a hopeful smile. "However, come see what I have planned!" He jumped up from his seat and headed out of the kitchen. Hubert finished the last of his orange juice and followed.

"There," said his father proudly as they reached the living room. He gestured grandly toward the fireplace. "Now we don't need a chimney sweep!" His chest swelled like a pouter pigeon. He smiled so that the evening sunlight glinted off a small gold filling in one tooth. "That way, we shall entice your mother back without having to waste money."

Hubert glanced from his father to the fireplace. It was entirely closed over with copies of the *Pugford Chronicle* taped together. He suppressed a groan. Sometimes he wondered if his father was crazy as well as stupid. "That'll keep the soot in all right, Dad," he said, "but what about when we have to light a fire?"

His father gave him a long-suffering look. "It's not to keep the soot in. It's the first step in Operation Get Madge Back." He paused dramatically. "We are going to sweep the chimney *ourselves!*"

A light bulb went on in Hubert's head and he saw the rods against the wall by the back door. His father had been forced to buy them a year ago when the drains got blocked. They had come complete with chimney brushes at no extra cost. In the present moment his father had obviously remembered them. Hubert stared at the sealed fireplace. "How do you get the brush up?"

"We don't," his father said promptly. "That's the trick. We do it from the roof! That way, you don't put the brushes up at all. You push them *down*. The whole fireplace stays completely sealed with newspapers, thus trapping the soot inside and avoiding a mess." He smiled broadly. "Once the chimney's clean, I'll ring your mother and tell her to come home. It'll probably be *years* before any more soot falls down." He looked benignly at Hubert. "If you do it now, you should have time to take a shower before dinner."

"Do what?" Hubert asked. He felt suddenly cold.

"Go up on the roof and sweep the chimney," his father said. "I've left the ladder and the brushes in the rod case by the back door."

"I can't go up on the roof," Hubert told him quickly. "Because of my ears." He suffered from vertigo, a condition that meant heights made him dizzy. The doctor had once told him it came from the canals in his ears.

"Well *I* certainly can't do it," his father said. "Far too undignified at my age." He sniffed. "I'd have thought you'd make a special effort for your mother."

They bickered about it for another hour, while Hubert tried to do his homework, and continued to bicker about it while his father prepared supper. They were still arguing about it as they ate off trays on their knees in the living room. Hubert forked baked beans into his mouth, listlessly staring at the papered fireplace. In among the jumble of type he could see the headline that had caught his attention on the bus: HUMAN CANNONBALL FIRED. It occurred to him that life might be a lot simpler if he ran away to the circus and stayed there.

"You know," his father was saying, "most people believe vertigo is all in the mind. Now I know the doctor said—" He stopped as the front door bell rang. "It's your mother!" he exclaimed excitedly. "She's come back. I knew she would. Hurry up and let her in!"

But it wasn't Hubert's mother. It was Slider Coffrey. He stood at the front door holding a greasy brown paper bag. Behind him was a homemade wagon piled high with the most astonishing assortment of junk Hubert had ever seen. "Come on," Slider said. "It's time for you to get turned into a human cannonball."

CHAPTER SIX

Down at the bottom of the back garden, Slider opened the brown paper bag and took out a hot dog covered with mustard and ketchup. He bit the end off it. "Want one?" he asked Hubert, offering the bag. "There's a couple of cheeseburgers in there as well."

"Thanks," Hubert said. His father's suppers would hardly fill a tooth. He took a lucky dip into the bag and came up with a cheeseburger. It tasted divine. "What you got on the cart, Slider?"

Slider tapped the side of his nose and grinned. "Your cannon, sort of. I'll show you." He finished off the hot dog and set the bag carefully to one side. He took two cans of Coke from a side pocket, handed one to Hubert, and jerked the ring-pull of the other. He tipped his head back and drank with all the satisfaction of someone appearing in a commercial. After a moment he belched lightly, set the Coke down, and took the second hot dog from the bag. "I couldn't get a cannon," he said between bites, as if it was a minor oversight, "so I decided we'd use a rocket."

Hubert finished his cheeseburger. "What's a rocket got to do with it?"

"Well," said Slider, "you want to be able to say you've had *experience* as a human cannonball. So what does a human cannonball do?"

"He gets shot out of a cannon," Hubert said, puzzled.

"He flies through the air!" Slider corrected him triumphantly. When Hubert still looked blank, he added, "And what does a rocket do? *It* flies through the air!"

Hubert popped his Coke and drank some to disguise the fact that he didn't know what Slider was talking about. Apparently he didn't succeed very well, for Slider said with long-suffering patience, "So if we put *you* in the rocket, then *you* will also fly through the air. That way, you can say you've had *experience*."

"Oh, *that* sort of rocket!" Hubert exclaimed. He'd been thinking of the kind you set off when you had fireworks. "A rocket you can fly in!" He looked at the junk pile on the wagon. "Where is it?"

"We have to build it," Slider said easily. "I've got all the parts."

You could have fooled Hubert. The stuff on Slider's cart looked a long way from Cape Canaveral. He leaned over and poked. The biggest single item was an oil drum with the top cut off. The rest seemed to consist of a stout wooden plank, two round logs, some string, a length of thin wire, and a can of spray paint. Not for the first time he marveled at Slider's ability to put his hands on the most unlikely items. "This is it?" he asked, certain he was missing something.

"That's it," said Slider confidently. "Do you want that other cheeseburger?"

Hubert shook his head and watched in mild disbelief as it joined the two hot dogs. When he had finished, Slider said briskly, "Come on, you have to lend a hand—I can't build it by myself, you know."

"I don't know how you're going to build it at all," Hubert admitted.

"Every piece has its purpose," Slider told him. "But we have to proceed systematically. The first thing is to make sure you fit. Climb in the oil drum."

Hubert looked at Slider, then at the drum. "Is it clean?"

"Clean enough. There's no oil in it, if that's what you mean."

"It's just that my mom's left my dad," Hubert felt constrained to explain, "and I'll have to wash my own clothes if they get messed up."

"Oh," Slider said, not at all interested. He hauled the drum upright and peered inside it. "You should be all right."

Hubert climbed into the drum. He was not a particularly tall boy, but it only came up to the bottom of his chest.

"Scrunch down," Slider instructed. "You need to get the feel of what it's like in the barrel of a cannon."

Hubert scrunched down. It felt cramped and the drum gave off a strong metallic smell.

"I'm just going to throw my coat over the top so you can see what it feels like in the dark," Slider called.

Hubert waited, scrunched. In a moment, something covered the drum, cutting out much of the light. He looked around to find out if he could see anything and could not. But that actually made little difference, since he could see very little in the first place. After a moment, Slider removed the coat, and Hubert straightened up.

"How was it?" Slider asked him.

"Okay," Hubert said. He climbed out of the drum. There was some rust on his jacket, but it brushed off easily enough.

"All right," Slider said, "we'd better get this rocket off the ground."

"How are we going to do that?" Hubert asked.

"With these," Slider told him proudly. He rummaged through the remaining stuff on his wagon and produced from the bottom layer a brightly colored box Hubert hadn't noticed. He flipped the lid and held it out like somebody offering fancy chocolates.

Hubert looked inside. Six large fireworks rockets were packed neatly side by side. "Wow!" he said. "Where did you get those?"

"My dad had them hidden on the top shelf in the garage."

"Wow!" Hubert said again. "They're big."

"I think they're professional fireworks," Slider said. "You know, the ones they send up at displays. They work just the same as ordinary ones." He dug three out of the box and handed them to Hubert. "Come on, we have to get these tied to the drum."

It proved more difficult than it sounded. Slider insisted that the rockets should be placed evenly around the drum, so each one had to be tied individually. They ran out of string at the third rocket and out of wire at the fifth. For a moment it looked as though they would have to make do with five—and redistribute them around the drum. Then Hubert found some string in his pocket and, when that proved too short, added one of his own shoelaces.

When they were finished, Slider took up the can of spray paint and carefully wrote AEC on the side of the drum above the rockets.

"What's that mean?" Hubert asked him. He thought it might be some sort of code.

"Atomic Energy Commission," Slider told him.

Hubert inspected his atomic rocket. Even though the fireworks were large and there were six of them and even assuming they all went off at exactly the same time, he did not actually believe they would lift him and the heavy metal oil drum off the ground. What they might do, on the other hand, was cause the drum to get hot enough to fry him. "It won't work," he said.

To his surprise, Slider agreed. "Of course it won't—we haven't finished yet." He turned to give Hubert another of his patient long-suffering looks. "My father says it's all a question of thrust and escape velocity. We've got the thrust with the fireworks. Now we have to provide the escape velocity."

Hubert looked back at him suspiciously. Slider's father was a butcher, which hardly made him an expert on rocketry. All the same, he said, "How are we going to do that?"

"Give me a hand with this," said Slider, pointing at the plank.

Together they maneuvered the plank off the wagon. It was broad, thick, and surprisingly heavy. "Now these," said Slider, picking up the logs. He looked around him, as if inspecting the trees, then dropped the logs near the fence. "Fulcrum," he said mysteriously.

On Slider's instructions, they placed the plank across the logs to make what looked to Hubert like a seesaw, set in the shade of a chestnut tree. They positioned the oil drum so it sat on one end. "Here, wear this," Slider said, taking something else off the wagon. Hubert looked at it. It was a bicycle helmet. "Belongs to my sister," Slider explained. "She won't miss it." He sniffed, then added, "Should fit—she's got an enormous head."

Hubert put on the helmet and tied the strap underneath his chin. It was actually a bit big for him, but he voiced no complaint. His mind was on the oil drum rocket. He still did not see how it could possibly take off.

"Now, climb in," Slider said.

"Into the drum again?"

"Into the rocket," Slider confirmed. He was taking a box of matches out of his pocket.

As Hubert climbed into the drum, he began to wonder why he took orders from Slider so obediently. In his wildest dreams he could not imagine how this makeshift nightmare might take off. An earlier thought recurred. "Won't the rockets make the drum hot?" he asked.

"Air pressure will take care of that," Slider said confidently. "Scrunch down."

"What are you going to do?"

"Light the rockets," Slider said. "I've fixed the fuse so they'll all fire together. I hope."

"But you said the rockets won't work."

"I said the rockets won't work on their own," Slider corrected him patiently. "You're forgetting about escape velocity."

"Where do we get that?" Hubert asked. Now that it had come to the crunch, he was feeling worried.

"When I light the rockets," Slider said, "I'm going to climb that tree. When they catch, but just before they actually go off, I'm going to jump down onto the far end of the seesaw. That will provide the escape velocity. My weight will throw you and the drum up in the air. The rockets will carry you the rest of the way. Scrunch down." He struck a match. "Timing is everything."

Hubert scrunched down hurriedly, suddenly aware his heart was beating like a tom-tom. He could not believe he had let Slider talk him into this, but it seemed too late to back out now. There was a slight hissing noise from the first of the rockets. He looked up from his scrunched position and caught a glimpse of Slider climbing up the tree. A second, then a third hiss told him the next two rockets had caught. "Hurry up, Slider!" he shouted out in panic.

"Don't worry!" Slider's voice floated down from somewhere up above him.

The remaining three rockets caught and Hubert knew it was only a matter of seconds now before they fired. He decided at that moment that he didn't want to be a human cannonball after all. Suddenly the fact that the bicycle helmet didn't fit properly seemed hugely important. He started to unscrunch. "Hey, Slider—"

"Geronimo!" yelled Slider as he dropped from the tree.

Slider, a substantial boy, hit the far end of the seesaw at the exact instant all six rockets fired. Hubert felt as if a giant hand had seized him and was hurling him upward. There was a jumble of impressions as he and the oil drum sailed in a fiery arc high over the garden fence. The rocket was working better than their wildest dreams. He felt as if he had gone as high as a house, maybe higher. Momentary terror was replaced by sudden joy. So this was what it felt like to be a human cannonball! Then he was coming down and the terror returned. He suddenly realized where he was.

The fireworks fizzled out. The rocket dropped like a stone. Hubert was directly over the roof of Mrs. Pomfrey-Parkinson's brand-new garden shed.

CHAPTER SEVEN

There was a crash fit to wake the dead. The oil drum rocket, with Hubert inside, went directly through the roof to land in a shower of asbestos shingles on the floor. The drum overturned and Hubert sprawled out, skinning his knees and banging his elbow. His head struck something hard, but fortunately the cycling helmet absorbed most of the shock. There was a moment of confusion, then he clambered to his feet.

He was still dazed. His head seemed to turn a

complete circle if he moved it suddenly, but apart from a few scrapes he seemed in one piece. After a moment, cautiously, he looked around.

The first thing he saw was his soccer ball, still lying on the floor where he had spotted it the day before. The next thing he saw was the weird machine.

It was even bigger and far more peculiar than he remembered it. Through the window he had had an impression of gleaming chrome and twisting tubes. Close up he could now see a tangle of electrical cables at the base and what looked vaguely like a computer keyboard, except there were fewer keys. Even stranger, each one was enormous, without a letter on it, and of a different color.

Above the keyboard was what he took to be a screen—but a screen like nothing he had ever seen before. It was round and slightly bulbous, like a giant, jet-black eye. The surface had a liquid sheen, but the most peculiar thing of all was the way it seemed so deep. When he looked at that screen, his gaze seemed to go on and on. Tiny pinpoints of colored lights flickered within it, as if he was staring at distant stars in the cold depths of space.

The tiny lights winked on and off. Hubert did not want to take his eyes off the screen, could not take his eyes off the screen, could not, even with an effort, take his eyes off the screen. He found himself swaying. His thoughts slowed. It was as if his mind was being drawn into the screen, drawn toward those distant, flickering lights. He began to walk forward, like a robot.

There was the rattle of a handle, then a loud knocking from outside. Hubert stopped, the spell broken. He turned away from the screen and his mind snapped like a rubber band that's been stretched and let go.

"Hubert? Are you in there? Are you all right?" It was Slider's voice, sounding anxious.

"I think so," Hubert said. He felt dazed, but he expected that was the way he should feel after flying in his cannonball rocket. Dazed or not, he knew whose shed he was in. "Can you get me out?"

The handle of the shed door rattled briefly again. "It's locked," Slider said. "You'll have to open it from the inside."

Hubert walked over and tried. Some locks opened easily from the inside, but this wasn't one of them. He looked about for a key. "I can't," he called. "There's no key in here."

"What about the window? Can you get out through the window?"

Hubert glanced across. The window, which had been open the day before, was now firmly shut. He noticed the steely glint of a security lock. Mrs. Pomfrey-Parkinson had obviously decided she wanted no more nosy boys peering into her shed. "No," he told Slider, "that's locked, too."

There was a lengthy pause, then Slider said, "I don't suppose you could get out through the roof?"

It was an interesting idea. Hubert looked up. The hole in the roof was certainly big enough for him to climb through—after all, he'd made it himself. The problem was reaching it. "Hold on a minute," he called to Slider. He went over to the oil drum and stood it on its end. He climbed on the drum and reached up. He was still a good eighteen inches short.

"What are you doing?" Slider asked from outside.

"Just seeing if I can get out through the roof."

"Well, hurry up—I don't like it here." Slider obviously knew Mrs. Pomfrey-Parkinson's reputation.

Hubert climbed down off the oil drum. There was no sign of a ladder in the shed, and the only other thing he could stand on was the mysterious machine. But even if he'd been prepared to risk that, it was in the wrong place. Or the hole was in the wrong place, depending on how you looked at it. Anyway, he could see without even trying that it would be impossible to reach the hole by standing on the weird machine. "It's not going to work," he told Slider.

"You can't just stay in there," Slider said unnecessarily. "She'll kill you if she finds you."

Hubert suspected it was true, but didn't know what to do about it. He started to wonder about breaking the window. It would be a dreadful thing to do, and since he'd already broken the roof, he'd probably be put in jail. But even that might be better than waiting for the dreaded Mrs. Pomfrey-Parkinson to find him. Not that breaking the window would be all that easy. Glass only smashed easily when you didn't want it to. Besides, if Mrs. Pomfrey-Parkinson locked her shed, the window might be made of security glass, which was as breakable as steel.

"Hey!" Slider called excitedly.

"What?"

"I've just been looking at this lock. My dad has one just like it—he got it for the back door when there were all those burglaries, but he never got around to putting it on. Maybe his key will fit this one!"

Hubert felt a sudden surge of hope. It was possible. "Hey, Slider, that's a great idea!"

"I'll go get it!" Slider said. "I'll be back in ten minutes if I run all the way. You stay there."

You stay there, Hubert thought. As if he was likely to be going anywhere. "Just hurry," he called to Slider. But there was no reply. Slider had already gone.

Hubert glanced nervously back at the strange machine. At first he took great care not to look directly at that bulbous round black screen, but after a moment he discovered he could do so safely. It was no longer drawing him toward it, although the little lights still winked in its depths.

It struck him as very odd that Mrs. Pomfrey-Parkinson had a machine like this in her garden shed. But the real mystery was what the machine was *for*. The screen and keyboard made him think it might be some sort of computer, but what sort of computer had no letters or numbers on its keys? And what sort of computer had a fish-eye screen with little lights winking on and off? And what sort of computer needed power cables thick enough to run a steelworks? Most of all, what sort of person would keep a working computer in their garden shed? It was crazy.

If it wasn't a computer, what else could it be? Slider had a friend called Brian whose father was a radio ham. Once Brian had brought Slider and Hubert to see his father's setup, which half filled a shack at the bottom of his garden. It had all seemed very strange and impressive, but Hubert could remember nothing that looked remotely like the thing standing in front of him now. Besides, Brian's father had an enormous antenna on the roof of the shack. There was nothing at all on the roof of Mrs. Pomfrey-Parkinson's shed, as Hubert had discovered when he fell through it.

So what was it?

Even though the screen with the winking lights was definitely not drawing him toward it, Hubert took a step forward. For some reason, his nervousness about the machine was dying away. It no longer looked as strange as it had done. In fact it was now looking quite familiar, almost friendly.

Hubert took another step forward. The little lights in the screen danced and twinkled merrily. He found himself smiling. He could not understand why he had been worried about the machine before. It was actually a rather interesting machine, a rather nice machine. Still smiling, Hubert moved closer.

The machine, which had been silent up to now, suddenly began to hum. It was the same sound he had heard yesterday, but now it no longer set his teeth on edge. It sounded rather pleasant, almost musical. The lights in the screen danced and winked as Hubert moved closer.

One of the colored keys began to glow.

A very strange thing happened to Hubert then. One of his eyes turned downward toward the glowing key, the other remained fixed on the winking lights in the fish-eye screen. It should have been painful, but wasn't. His eyes moved like well-oiled ball bearings. It did feel weird, though, because instead of seeing what he was looking at, he saw two different things at the same time.

Watching the screen and the glowing key, Hubert took another step forward.

He felt very relaxed and very happy. Even the

thought of Mrs. Pomfrey-Parkinson did not disturb him. The world was wonderful. It had a place for him and this marvelous machine. His right hand moved of its own accord and floated above the glowing key.

CHAPTER EIGHT

Smiling, Hubert pressed the key.

There was a weird, low ringing noise and a strong smell of ozone. His eyes snapped back into their normal positions. For an instant, his head seemed to turn inside out. There was a flash of light that shook reality, and then a shimmering. He felt as if he were falling, although he knew he was still standing in the same place. He had a brief glimpse of blazing suns and a planet with rings. Then the ringing noise stopped, and he was back in front of the strange machine.

Hubert jerked his hand off the glowing key. "Wow!" He shook his head and took a quick step backward. Maybe he should have been more careful. He certainly didn't want to do anything that would bring Mrs. Pomfrey-Parkinson down on him. And since he didn't know what the machine did, it might have set off alarm bells all over Pugford. Still, whatever it did, it had stopped doing it now. Even the key he had pressed was no longer glowing. No harm done. He turned away from the machine.

He was no longer in Mrs. Pomfrey-Parkinson's garden shed.

Hubert spun around. The machine was still there and it looked like the same machine. But this was definitely not the same place. He was in a large chamber, far larger than the shed, with metal walls, floor and ceiling. There was no hole in the roof, no window at all. The room was lit, but he could not see from where. If anything, the whole place seemed to be glowing slightly.

He looked around, dumbstruck. There was a chair to one side of the machine. At least he thought it was a chair, although it was twisted and distorted like no chair he'd ever seen; whatever sat in it would have to have three rear ends. Beyond the chair was a table, definitely a table. Except it had no legs. The tabletop, of some thick, transparent material, floated in midair about three feet above the floor. On the table was a vase of flowers. Three of them turned toward him and wriggled.

Hubert shuddered. He could see a padded couch attached to one wall, but it was sloped in such a way you were bound to slide off if you tried to sit on it. To one side of the couch was what might have been a beanbag chair, except it seemed to be breathing. In the middle of the chamber, metallic tentacles hung down from the ceiling. They waved and twisted gently, like seaweed under water.

There was a two-foot cube on the floor near where his soccer ball had lain in the shed. Its sides were alternately black and white and he had no idea what it might be used for. Two of the walls were hung with pictures—what a relief to spot something familiar—in circular frames. Each showed a mountain landscape with high, thin, impossible peaks. The predominant color was pink and the foothills of the mountains were strewn with rubbish.

There were three doors—he hoped they were doors, he prayed they were doors. All were far wider than a normal door, but none was more than five feet high. Set into each door was a gently glowing panel.

Hubert gulped.

For a long moment he simply stood, his heartbeat pounding in his ears, his mind a whirl of utter confusion. Where was he? More important, how had he got there? Most important, how was he going to get back? He wished Slider was with him. He wished his father was with him. He even wished *Janice* was with him.

Most of all, he wished he was somewhere else.

He darted for the nearest door and pushed. Nothing happened. There was no handle on the door, no knob. He tried pushing it sideways. Still nothing happened. He had a feeling the control—if there was a control—might be the glowing panel, but he was afraid to touch it. The last time he'd touched anything that glowed— the key on the weird machine—he'd ended up here. All the same, if he didn't touch the glowing panel, his chances of getting out of here seemed slim. He touched the glowing panel. The door made a small chuckling noise, but nothing else happened. He touched it again, the barest brush of his fingertips. Again the chuckling noise and nothing else.

In a sudden surge of courage, Hubert placed his whole palm flat on the glowing panel and pressed firmly. The door slid open with a soft hiss. Behind it was a cupboard with five shelves of translucent tubes. Shadowy things moved slowly inside them.

Hubert backed away hurriedly, and the door slid shut of its own accord. He took a deep breath to steady his nerves and told himself that at least he'd found the secret to opening the doors. He went quickly to the second of them and pressed his hand flat on the glowing panel. It opened into another room, smaller than the one he was in and empty of anything except another of those breathing beanbags squatting in the middle of the floor. This one was a lot larger than the one he'd just seen, as if it was designed for sleeping, not just sitting. On the far wall was another of the glowing panels, but one which did not seem to be attached to any door.

He ducked down, walked in, and the door slid shut behind him. In a moment of panic he swung around, convinced he must be trapped. But there was a glow panel on the inside as well and the door opened again at a touch of his hand. Reassured he would not be trapped, he crossed the room, carefully skirting the breathing bean-bag, and stared up at the panel on the wall. After a moment he placed his hand on it.

The entire wall disappeared.

Hubert felt his jaw drop, but could do nothing about it. He was staring out into the velvet darkness of space, sprinkled with a billion stars. For some reason they did not twinkle, but glowed like still, perfect diamonds, pinpoints of steady light. Below him was a huge blue-and-white ball, the most beautiful sight he'd ever seen. It appeared to be moving—slowly, but very definitely moving.

He stared fascinated at the great blue ball. But at the same time something nibbled at the edges of his mind, something about stars that didn't twinkle. Some lesson at school, some book he'd read said the only stars that didn't twinkle weren't stars at all, but planets. That was the way you could tell the difference. But it wasn't that. There were only nine planets in the whole solar system and there were literally millions of stars out there that didn't twinkle. Why didn't the stars twinkle? And what was the big, blue—?

He had it! The memory came crashing in on him. What he'd read was that *no* stars really twinkled. They only *seemed* to twinkle because you were looking at them through the atmosphere. Once you got above the earth's atmosphere and looked at the stars, they didn't twinkle at all. Once you got—

Hubert gulped again. He seemed to be doing a lot of gulping lately, but he couldn't really blame himself in the circumstances. He was looking at the stars from outside the earth's atmosphere! Which meant—

He looked down slowly and this time recognized the huge blue-and-white ball spinning far below him. He had a poster of that same blue ball on the wall of his bedroom at home. They'd made the poster from a color photograph of the planet that the Apollo astronauts had taken from the moon. Hubert felt his head reel. There was only one explanation possible. He was in some sort of spaceship in orbit around Earth.

CHAPTER NINE

Hubert fell back like the heroine in a Victorian melodrama, and he was suddenly looking at a blank wall again. He was in space! He, Hubert Baker, was actually standing in a spaceship! It was impossible, but it was happening. How on earth had he got there?

Something nudged the back of his leg and he glanced down to find the breathing beanbag had crawled across the floor and was now rubbing his ankle like a friendly cat. He felt an almost overwhelming urge to lie down but fought it off. He was beginning to get the hang of these strange machines and objects. Somehow each of them encouraged you to use it. The glowing panels had enticed him to place his hand flat. The bed—he was sure now that the beanbag was some sort of alien bed—actually *wanted* him to rest. The weird machine in Mrs. Pomfrey-Parkinson's shed had somehow persuaded him to press one of its keys.

What had happened when he pressed the key? Hubert thought he knew the answer to that one too. "Beam me up, Scottie"—that's what had happened. The weird machine in Mrs. Pomfrey-Parkinson's shed had to be some sort of transporter, like they had on *Star Trek*. The thing next door wasn't the same machine at all. It was a receiver.

Hubert placed his hand on the door panel, ducked down, and walked back into the other room. He almost tripped over the breathing beanbag chair, which had crawled after him when he left the room, presumably in the hope he would like to sit down. Hubert ignored it. The transporter-receiver stood in the same place, little lights winking and blinking out of its fish-eye screen. There was one question left unanswered: What was Mrs. Pomfrey-Parkinson doing with a transporter in her garden shed?

There was only one door that Hubert hadn't tried, and he tried it now. It slid open at the touch of his palm on the panel and led into a well-lit corridor. Hubert stared in with a feeling of excitement and delight. Not only was he on a spaceship, he was on a *large* spaceship—maybe even a starship. This was even better than joining the circus. A lot better.

It turned out to be a smaller spaceship than he thought. There were only three doors along the corridor and one of them refused to open even when he placed his palm on the glowing panel. Of the other two, one opened into a room very similar to the room he'd just left, except it did not have a transporter machine. He walked to the last remaining door. It slid open with a hiss. Hubert ducked down and eagerly stepped inside. At once he wished he hadn't.

Mrs. Pomfrey-Parkinson was standing just inside the door.

She looked even more sinister than the last time he saw her. For one thing she wasn't just standing, she was hunched over, with her arms trailing like a gorilla and her head jutting forward. Her eyes were wide and staring and oddly colorless. Most horrible of all, she wasn't wearing any clothes. She looked like an awesome version of the old ad for auto tires, the Michelin Man.

Hubert averted his eyes and did a quick about-face. "I'm terribly sorry, Mrs. Pomfrey-Parkinson," he said over his shoulder. "I didn't know this was your roo—I didn't think you would be nu—dressing. I didn't—" He trailed off in a sort of strangled gurgle. Mrs. Pomfrey-Parkinson said nothing.

Hubert cleared his throat, still with his back to her. It was a dangerous position, since she might decide to strangle him with her bare hands, but at the same time he could hardly walk off and close the door without an explanation. After all, he *was* trespassing on her spaceship. "The thing is, Mrs. Pomfrey-Parkinson," he said, "I wanted to go to the circus and my dad wouldn't give me the money so I decided to become a human cannonball because they fired the other one and my friend Slider made this rocket to give me experience and that's why I'm here. That's also why I'm wearing a bicycle helmet." He'd purposely skirted the business about the shed. He thought he might get around to explaining that a little later.

Mrs. Pomfrey-Parkinson said nothing.

Hubert stole a quick glance over his shoulder, mainly to make sure she wasn't creeping up on him. But Mrs. Pomfrey-Parkinson hadn't moved. She was still standing in that peculiar hunched over position, arms trailing, face vacant. Then he saw the wires.

Hubert turned very, very slowly. Mrs. Pomfrey-Parkinson wasn't standing inside the door at all—she was hanging from wires attached to the ceiling. There was a wire to her head and a wire to each shoulder. For one terrifying instant he thought she might be dead, then realized it was far more awesome than that. What he was looking at wasn't Mrs. Pomfrey-Parkinson at all—it was some sort of freaked-out bodysuit.

Cautiously Hubert circled the bodysuit. It looked exactly like Mrs. Pomfrey-Parkinson (so far as he could tell without her clothes on) but when you got around to the back you could see it was a blubbery shell that lay open and hollow all along the spine. You put it on like some sort of coverall and when it was on, you looked like Mrs. Pomfrey-Parkinson.

The room was small, little more than a cupboard. Hubert backed away from the Mrs. Pomfrey-Parkinson suit with a distinct feeling of disgust. There was something quite awful about this blubbery suit hanging from wires. The stuff it was made from looked horribly real, fat and squishy, like Mrs. Pomfrey-Parkinson herself. Worse still, it had a fishy smell.

Something made him reach out to touch it. At once the suit began to wrap around his hand, as if trying to absorb it. Hubert jerked his hand away in horror. The suit was like the breathing beanbags and the transporter machine—it *wanted* him to put it on. He had a horrid vision of himself absorbed by the suit, looking like the loathsome Mrs. Pomfrey-Parkinson. Shuddering, he went back to the door.

But he hesitated before leaving. Nothing was making much sense, but this blubber suit was making the least sense of all. He palmed the panel and went out. He was frowning in deep thought all the way back down the corridor and still frowning as he returned to the first room he had entered. The breathing beanbag had crawled across the floor and was waiting for him immediately inside, but he kicked it to one side.

As he walked across the room, he pondered. There was a spaceship orbiting Earth and somehow, miraculously, he was on it. Where had it come from? Something told him he could rule out the Americans, and he was fairly sure he'd read somewhere that the Russians weren't sending up rockets anymore. Besides—he hesitated to think it, then thought it anyway—nothing about this ship felt really human. The doors were too small and the wrong shape. The things in it—like the breathing beanbags—were like nothing he'd ever heard of.

But if it wasn't a human ship, what was it? Alien, whispered the voice inside his head. This one's come to pick up ET. You're flying in a vessel of the Klingon Empire. For once Hubert didn't tell the voice to shut up. He had an uneasy suspicion that what it was saying was exactly right. He had boarded something built by beings from another planet.

Was there anybody—any*thing*, his mind corrected him—else on the ship? He didn't think so. He'd seen nothing else, except the stupid beanbags, which might have been alive and might not. Besides that, one of the doors had been locked. It might have led to a cupboard or a fuel room, but it might also have led into a corridor a mile long. He had no idea how big the ship really was or what lay beyond the door. So he could be alone, or he could be sharing the vessel with a thousand aliens.

The thought took him back to the transporter. If there were a thousand aliens on the ship, he didn't think he wanted to meet them. He thought he wanted to get back promptly to Pugford. Hope you remember how to work the transporter, murmured that hard-bitten voice in his head.

Had it been the green key or the blue key? And if he picked the same key, would that make the machine send him back to Earth? For all he knew, it might set up a transmission link to the aliens' home planet circling Alpha Centauri. But as if that wasn't enough to be worrying about, his mind kept wrestling with the problem of why Mrs. Pomfrey-Parkinson had a transporter to an alien spaceship in her garden shed. Nothing, absolutely nothing, made any sense.

He pressed the green key.

There was the same low ringing noise and smell of ozone. His head seemed to turn inside out again. Then there was the flash and the shimmering, the feeling of falling. The ringing stopped.

Hubert looked around quickly and felt relief flood over him like a tidal wave. He'd made the round trip safely. He was back in the shed. What's more, somebody was jiggling a key in the lock.

"Hey, Slider!" he called out excitedly. "You'll never believe what the old cow's got in here!"

But when the shed door opened, it wasn't Slider.

CHAPTER TEN

Hubert pasted on his widest, most ingratiating smile. It made him look like a panic-stricken sheep. "You must be wondering, Mrs. Pomfrey-Parkinson," he said, "what I'm doing in your shed. Well, I can explain everything. The thing was, I wanted to go to the circus and my father wouldn't let me have the money, so I thought I'd be their new human cannonball because they fired the old one and my friend Slider—"

"Shut up," said Mrs. Pomfrey-Parkinson.

Hubert shut up. Mrs. Pomfrey-Parkinson had always been scary, but now there was something about her that made him feel he was caught in a crypt with Count Dracula. She still looked the same—

Like the blubber suit hanging from wires in a spaceship orbiting Earth!

—and she still smelled the same, a cloud of perfume, talcum powder, and cologne—

To hide the smell of fish!

—but even though her eyes weren't flashing red, they were dark and cold and threatening as the eyes of a crocodile. They flickered like a reptile's tongue to the weird machine and back. "You've used it, haven't you?" said Mrs. Pomfrey-Parkinson.

"Used it? Used what? Oh, that! No, of course I—well, not exactly *used*, more like—well, actually, of course I—yes. Yes, I used it," Hubert said. If his life depended on it, he seemed incapable of telling a lie. And your life probably did depend on it, muttered the voice in his head resignedly.

"Come with me!" Mrs. Pomfrey-Parkinson's hand shot out and clamped like a vise on Hubert's arm. She jerked him toward her.

Hubert tried to resist. He was a chunky boy, not particularly tall for his age, but toughened by soccer and his training as a human cannonball. He might as well have been a dandelion for all the good it did him. Being jerked by Mrs. Pomfrey-Parkinson was like being tied to a tank.

Hubert snapped forward, collided with her ample bosom, and bounced slightly. She felt exactly like the blubber suit, and this close he could definitely smell fish under the cloud of perfume. He tried to pull away, but she held him like a hawser. She turned and dragged him from the shed along the path into the house.

The house was another surprise. Hubert remembered it from the days when Mr. Willis lived there. Then it had been very neat and clean and smelled of polish. But now, as he was dragged into the living room, he found himself in a cross between a junk shop and a trash dump. There were rusting cans strewn on the floor; old Chinese take-out cartons; half-eaten, rotting fruit; yellowing vegetables; bits of paper; empty bottles—it went on and on. The smell made him gag.

Mrs. Pomfrey-Parkinson shoved him into a rickety wooden chair. "Sit," she said.

Hubert sat. He was too terrified to do anything

else. A horrible suspicion had solidified into certainty. Mrs. Pomfrey-Parkinson wasn't Mrs. Pomfrey-Parkinson. Mrs. Pomfrey-Parkinson wasn't even human. Mrs. Pomfrey-Parkinson was something from beyond the farthest reaches of the solar system, wearing a blubber suit disguised to make it *appear* human.

The Thing in the Mrs. Pomfrey-Parkinson blubber suit turned toward him and smiled, as if reading his thoughts. "You're right," it said. "I must congratulate you—you're the first to suspect. I thought we would have taken over all of Pugford before we had to deal with anything like this."

"We?" Hubert echoed, staring at the Mrs. Pomfrey-Parkinson Thing.

"Exiles from the planet Tenalp in the Metsys system."

"Exiles?" Hubert echoed. "Why are you exiles?"

"Our planet grew too polluted for us to live on it," the Thing said shortly.

Looking around Mrs. Pomfrey-Parkinson's living room, Hubert could see why. Diplomatically he said, "So you're looking for another planet to move onto?"

"To take over," the Thing corrected him. "We're not sharing a planet with anyone. Hence the plan."

"The plan?" echoed Hubert. He was doing quite a lot of echoing, but he couldn't seem to stop himself.

"The plan to conquer Earth," the Mrs. Pomfrey-Parkinson Thing said. "First, I stay in Pugford to find out how soft the native Earthlings really are. If there's no trouble, I signal the start of phase two."

"Phase two?" Hubert echoed. Briefly he thought of biting his tongue.

"A large group of our people move in, disguised as a traveling circus," the Mrs. Pomfrey-Parkinson Thing smiled grimly. "As you can see, we have no problem looking like human beings. Before anyone realizes what is happening we will have taken over Pugford." It giggled. "Once we have set up base in Pugford, we will gradually take over all of Britain. Then we will declare war on America and when we have won that, we will conquer the rest of the world!" To Hubert's horror, the Thing began to hum "Land of Hope and Glory." "The war shouldn't last more than a week or so. Our weaponry is much superior."

"War?" Hubert echoed. This Thing was talking about a war that would wipe out all human life on the planet. He had to get away and tell somebody.

"You have no chance of getting away," said the Mrs. Pomfrey-Parkinson Thing reading his mind again. "I am not at all what I seem, as I know you know. Beneath this humanoid disguise lies a million years of alien evolution. I could rip you apart before you'd taken three steps."

Hubert suspected it was all too true, so he stayed where he was, trying to come up with an escape plan without actually thinking about escaping. It wasn't easy.

"However," said the Mrs. Pomfrey-Parkinson Thing, its eyes flashing red, "the plan is still vulnerable at this stage. There are some common Earth substances that can do us great harm—simple carbon, for example. Unless I show I can successfully take over Pugford, the Grand Council will call off the invasion and search for another planet. Since our so-called circus won't be moving in until Saturday, I have to keep my real identity secret until then. And to do that, I shall have to do away with you."

Behind the Thing, the door crashed open. "Oh no, you don't!" came a familiar voice. Slider burst into the room carrying a plastic phaser from a "Star Trek" set. It looked good and made a funny noise, but all it fired was a flashlight beam. "What I have in my hand is a sonic disrupter," he exclaimed, "which will blow you to atoms at a touch of this button. Furthermore, I have already told everyone in Pugford of your evil plan and called the police. They should be arriving any second, so you just be a sensible alien and let my friend Hubert—"

"It's no good, Slider," Hubert told him wearily. "It's telepathic. It can read your mind."

"Oh," Slider said.

The Mrs. Pomfrey-Parkinson Thing took the phaser from Slider and crushed it into plastic granules with one hand. Then it pushed Slider roughly into another chair and kicked the living-room door closed. "So now," it said, "the two of you must die!"

To Hubert's horror, the Mrs. Pomfrey-Parkinson Thing reached up and split its own head open from crown to chin with a painted fingernail. Its whole face fell away in two neat halves. Its throat began to open lengthwise. It wriggled and the blubber suit slid in a quivering heap onto the floor.

"Good grief!" Slider gasped. He looked ready to pass out.

What emerged from the blubber suit was almost indescribable. It was a cross between a Komodo dragon and a giant stick insect with patches of near luminous bluebottle skin. It had fangs. It had tentacles. It had long, thin, hairy legs. It had red eyes. It started to shuffle slowly toward the boys.

"How are we going to get out of this?" Slider muttered.

Hubert didn't answer. Hubert didn't know.

CHAPTER ELEVEN

The Thing shuffled forward, tentacles waving, fangs snapping, eyes flashing. Hubert knew he was going to have to fight. What he didn't know was how he was going to win. He'd felt how strong the Thing was, even in the Mrs. Pomfrey-Parkinson blubber suit. There was a large vase in the corner he might use to bonk it over its triangular head, but to get to the vase he had to get past the Thing itself, which was impossible. Outside of the movies, life never worked out right.

The Thing reached for Hubert.

A vast black cloud erupted from the fireplace and billowed through the room. The Thing gave a piercing scream and began to wave its tentacles in sudden panic. "Carbon!" it gasped. It seemed to be having trouble breathing.

Hubert was out of his chair like a human cannonball. "Come on, Slider!" he yelled. Then without waiting to find out if Slider had obeyed, he dived past the thrashing Thing and grabbed the vase. As he spun around, he saw that Slider had not been so lucky. A snaking tentacle was wrapped around his ankle. Although the Thing looked in deep trouble, it was still holding him firmly.

Another cloud erupted from the fireplace.

"Eeeeeagh!" screamed the Thing.

Hubert, face and hands now black as pitch, brought the vase down on the Mrs. Pomfrey-Parkinson Thing's pointed head. The vase shattered, and the Thing disappeared.

"Thanks," Slider said as his ankle was freed.

Hubert was standing staring stupidly at the spot where the Thing had been. There were bits of broken vase all over the place, but not a hint of the Thing itself—no insides, no green blood, no bits of tentacle, nothing. It was as if the creature had never been.

"What did you do?" asked Slider.

Hubert didn't know. He supposed he must have killed it, but he was far from certain. Where was the body? One minute the creature had been there, choking on the soot from the fireplace, the next it was simply gone. It was crazy. There was no—

Then it hit him. "I didn't do anything!" he screamed at Slider. "It's gone back to its ship! This room's full of soot and it couldn't stand the carbon, so it beamed itself aboard the way they do on *Star Trek*! Come on!" He started from the room.

"Where are we going?" Slider gasped.

"To the shed!" Hubert told him. "That's where it keeps the transporter machine. We have to get to the ship and stop it signaling for the circus to move in, otherwise the whole world is doomed!"

"But we can't stop it!" Slider protested. "You saw what it was like—it could eat the two of us alive! The only thing that's stopped it so far is it doesn't like the taste of soot!"

Hubert stared at his friend in admiration. "Slider," he said, "you're a genius."

In a few moments they were pounding down

the garden path together, a bulging trash bag bouncing on Hubert's back. They crashed into the garden shed.

"Don't look at the screen," Hubert muttered.

"How does it work?" asked Slider.

"You press this," Hubert said, thumping a fist down on the big green key.

"It's just humming," Slider protested. "We haven't gone anywhere."

"Look around you," Hubert told him shortly.

They were in the ship all right, but the room was empty. Hubert ran to the exit door and slapped his hand on the panel. Together they ran out into the corridor. The door at the end, the one that had previously been locked, now stood open. "Through there!" Hubert screamed. He ran without waiting to find if Slider was following.

Together they crashed through the doorway into what was obviously a control deck. There were banks of machinery built into the walls, control columns rising from the floor, and winking lights everywhere. One whole wall was transparent, giving a mind-blowing view of deep space with its blaze of stars.

"Wow!" Slider gasped.

But Hubert had no time for the view. His eyes

had locked on the Mrs. Pomfrey-Parkinson Thing, which was hunched over a control panel punching buttons with every one of its seven tentacles. It was screaming in some strange language.

"It's trying to call home!" Hubert shouted. "We have to stop it!"

The Thing swung around at the sound of his voice. "Keep away from me, puny humans, or I will tear you limb from limb!"

A crackling voice suddenly sounded out of a hidden speaker. It seemed to be giving a command.

The Mrs. Pomfrey-Parkinson Thing swung back to the controls.

Hubert reached the Thing in a single stride and dumped the trash bag of soot directly on its pointy head.

"Eeeeeaaaagh!" it wailed. Its tentacles waved wildly. Smoke curled out of the holes where a human's ears would be. Its body began to dissolve into putrid green slime.

The crackling voice sounded again. Something had to be done at once.

Whatever was at the other end might understand English since the Thing did. Hubert leaned forward. "There is extreme danger on Earth for our kind," he said in a fair imitation of the Thing's voice. "Under no circumstances should we continue our plans for an invasion."

"Message received and understood," the crackling voice acknowledged crisply.

"Nooooo!" wailed the Mrs. Pomfrey-Parkinson Thing. Then it formed a small puddle on the spaceship floor before evaporating in a fishy cloud.

CHAPTER TWELVE

"I did it myself!" Hubert's father announced as Hubert walked into the living room. He tossed his head. "Undignified though it was, I climbed onto the roof and used the brushes." He frowned slightly. "The only thing is, no soot seems to have come down." He gestured toward the fireplace from which he had removed the taped newspapers. It was empty.

"You brushed the wrong chimney," Hubert told him wearily. "That's why no soot came down. You put the brushes down Mrs. Pomfrey-Parkinson's chimney next door."

"What?" his father exclaimed. A look of panic clamped itself onto his features. "Mrs. Pomfrey-Parkinson will kill me!"

Not any more, Hubert thought. Aloud he said, "I think it'll be all right. Mrs. Pomfrey-Parkinson has moved out."

"Has she?" His father looked relieved. Then a frown crept back. "But that means I haven't swept *our* chimney—and I've already phoned your mother and told her to come home."

"If you put the papers back, *I'll* sweep our chimney tomorrow morning," Hubert said. Somehow climbing on the roof didn't seem such a big deal after looking down on Earth from outer space.

"Will you?" his father said delightedly. "Will you really? I'd be very grateful." He hesitated. "Of course, you realize this doesn't mean I can afford to give you any money for the circus."

"I don't think the circus will be coming to Pugford after all," said Hubert.

"That's good," his father said, relieved. He seemed to see Hubert properly for the first time and frowned again. "Why are you so dirty? What have you been doing?"

"Just playing," Hubert said. "I'm going up now to take a shower."

As he stood in the steaming shower stall watching the stream of water rinse the last of the soot out of his hair, he kept replaying the adventure in his mind. A part of him wanted to tell the world what he had done, to boast about the way that he and Slider had saved the planet. But nobody would believe it without proof and the only proof that would convince them was tucked away in Mrs. Pomfrey-Parkinson's garden shed. That was something he didn't want to show anybody for a while. As long as it remained his and Slider's little secret, they had their own spaceship to visit any time they wanted. Maybe one day they could even learn to fly it!

He toweled himself dry and dressed again in clean clothes. No, he thought, better not mention anything to anyone. That way he and Slider got to keep their spaceship—at least until their luck ran out. The thought gave him an appetite—he hadn't eaten anything since Slider gave him the cheeseburger—and he wondered if there might be anything tucked away in the back of the refrigerator. He hurried down the stairs.

His cousin Janice was sitting in the kitchen,

clutching a tall glass of milk. "Oh, Hubert," she gasped at once, "Uncle Arnold told me Mrs. Pomfrey-Parkinson has gone away, and he's going to ask my daddy if I can look after Hassle, and I know it was all your doing somehow." She looked at him dewy-eyed. "You are my hero, Hubert," and she gave him a loving look.

Hubert groaned and headed for the refrigerator.